This book belongs to

To Mum
(And Clare Pearson, who knows a thing or two about a story ending)
M.C.

For Mark, a fully paid-up member of The Cloud Appreciation Society.
Happy cloud spotting, love from Alice
A.J.

THIS IS A BORZOI BOOK PUBLISHED BY ALFRED A. KNOPF

Text copyright © 2012 by Michael Catchpool
Jacket art and interior illustrations copyright © 2012 by Alison Jay
All rights reserved. Published in the United States by Alfred A. Knopf, an imprint of Random House Children's Books,
a division of Random House, Inc., New York. Originally published in slightly different form in Great Britain
as *Cloth from the Clouds* by Gullane Children's Books, London, in 2012.
Knopf, Borzoi Books, and the colophon are registered trademarks of Random House, Inc.

Visit us on the Web! www.randomhouse.com/kids

Educators and librarians, for a variety of teaching tools, visit us at
www.randomhouse.com/teachers

Library of Congress Cataloging-in-Publication Data
Catchpool, Michael.
The cloud spinner / by Michael Catchpool ; illustrations by Alison Jay. — 1st American ed.
p. cm.
Summary: When the king orders a boy to make him a huge wardrobe out of the clouds in the sky,
the boy warns him that it is more than he needs, but the king does not listen.
ISBN 978-0-375-87011-8 (trade) — ISBN 978-0-375-97011-5 (lib. bdg.) — ISBN 978-0-375-98739-7 (ebook)
[1. Fairy tales. 2. Kings, queens, rulers, etc.—Fiction. 3. Clouds—Fiction. 4. Weaving—Fiction.] I. Jay, Alison, ill. II. Title.
PZ8.C279Cl 2012   [E]—dc22   2011000894

The illustrations in this book were created using alkyd paint and crackle varnish on thick cartridge paper.

MANUFACTURED IN CHINA
March 2012   10 9 8 7 6 5 4 3 2 1   First American Edition
Random House Children's Books supports the First Amendment and celebrates the right to read.

The Cloud Spinner

by Michael Catchpool • illustrated by Alison Jay

Alfred A. Knopf ✦ New York

There was once a boy who could weave cloth from the clouds.

He had a spinning wheel and a loom on top of a hill.
As the clouds passed, with a whir of the wheel,
he would spin them into thread: gold in the morning
with the rising sun, white in the afternoon,
and crimson in the evening.

Just as his mother had taught him.

Then, with a clickety-clack of his loom,
he would weave the thread into cloth.
As he worked, he sang a simple tune his mother had taught him:
"Enough is enough and not one stitch more."

The boy was wise.

He spun just enough thread
and wove just enough cloth
to make two scarves.

One, of pure white, he wore
over his head when it was hot,
to protect him from the sun.

The other he wore when it was cold.
It was a twist and twirl of gold
and white and crimson,
soft as a mouse's touch and
warm as roasted chestnuts.

His mother had taught him well.

One chilly market day,
the boy walked down the hill,
a basket in his hand and his
scarf around his neck.

The market was full
of great excitement—
the King was on his way!

Soon the King rode grandly by,
hardly noticing the curtsies and cheers.
But what his greedy eyes did notice was the
wonderful scarf of gold and white and crimson!

"Tell me, boy, where can I get a scarf of such fine cloth?"
"Nowhere on earth," the boy replied.
"Then how did you get yours?" snapped the King.
"I made it," said the boy.
"Then you will make another for me . . .

. . .a longer one, much longer, for I am the King!"
But the boy said, "It would not be wise to have a long scarf
made from this cloth. Your Majesty does not need it."
"How dare you tell me what is wise!" shouted the King.
"I order you to make me my scarf!"

So the boy went home to the top of the hill and, with a whir of the wheel, began to spin.

He spun the clouds as they passed in the morning and were gold with the rising sun.

He spun in the afternoon as the clouds sailed past, white as snowdrifts.

He spun in the evening,
when the clouds were crimson.

Then, with a clickety-clack of the loom,
he wove the thread into a long, long scarf.

The King was overjoyed. His scarf was soft
as a mouse's touch and warm as roasted chestnuts.
"Now make me a cloak of this glorious cloth," he ordered.
"And dresses galore for the Queen and my daughter, the Princess!"

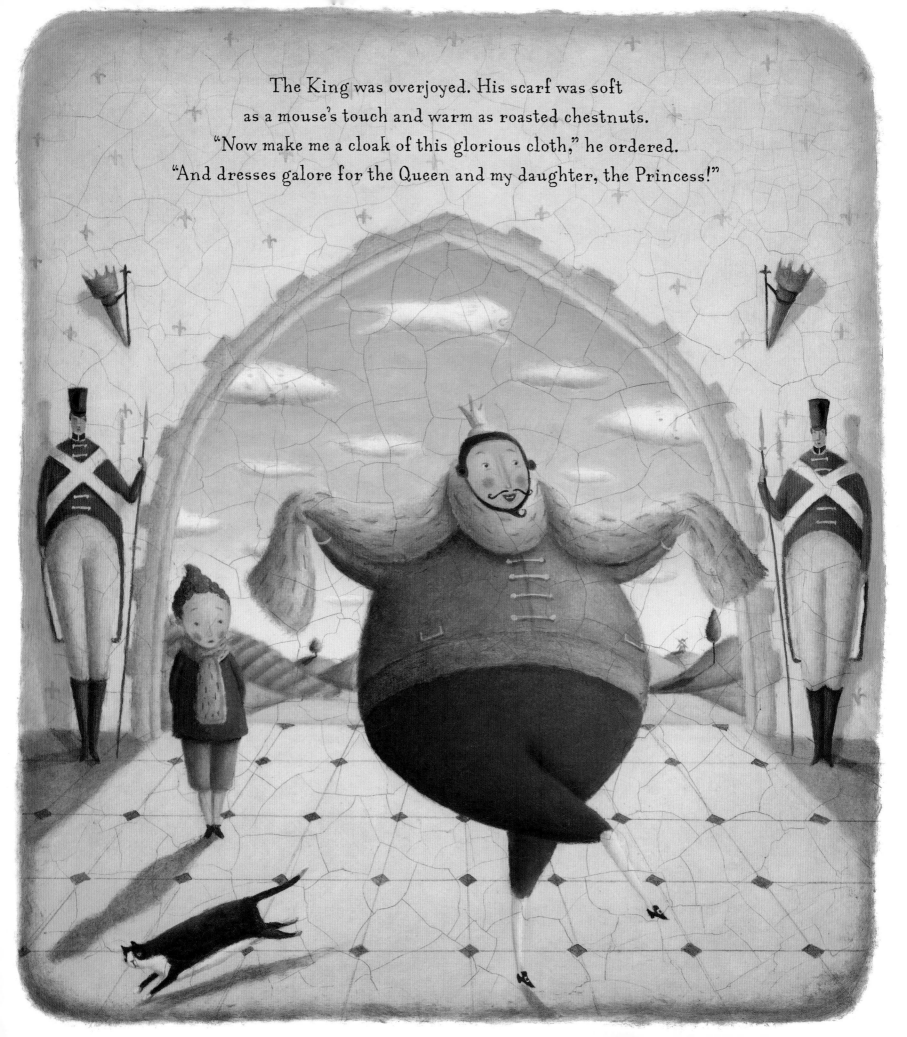

But the boy shook his head. "It would not be wise to have so many clothes made from this cloth. Your Majesty does not need them."

The King's face was a twist of scowls.
"I want those clothes and I order you to make them!"

So the boy went home to the top of the hill and,
with a whir of the wheel, began to spin.

He spun the clouds as they passed in the morning and were gold with the rising sun.

He spun in the afternoon as the clouds sailed past, white as snowdrifts.

And he spun in the evening, when the clouds were crimson.

He spun and he spun and it got harder and harder, for soon there were fewer and fewer clouds.

At last, with a clickety-clack of the loom, the boy began to weave the thread into cloth, beneath a cloudless sky.

And as he worked, he sadly sang,

"Enough is enough and not one stitch more."

The King was delighted.
He put on the wonderful cloak, and the Queen
and the Princess each put on a beautiful flowing dress.
"Surely," he boasted, "there is no other king
as magnificent and wise as me!"
"Not one!" said the Queen.

The Princess said nothing.

But day after day, as they wore their marvelous clothes,
not one drop of rain fell from the cloudless sky.

"Your Majesty," pleaded the villagers,
"our animals are thirsty and our crops are all dying."

"There's nothing I can do!" shouted the King,
walking this way and that, his cloak trailing behind him.
"Why are you moaning to me?"

The Princess said nothing . . .

But that evening, she quietly slipped out of the palace.
She wore a simple dress, and in her arms was a bundle,
soft as a mouse's touch and warm as roasted chestnuts.

She crossed the dry, dusty gardens and the brown fields
beyond, and climbed to the top of the hill.

Stepping forward,
she knocked at the boy's door.

"Is it too late to undo
what has been done?"

The boy smiled
and said simply . . .

"There is still time."

When the King awoke the next morning, he could not find his wonderful cloak. The Queen could not find her beautiful dresses. They searched the palace for the clothes that the boy had made, but they were gone.

While, outside, the villagers danced for joy as the rain began to fall from the clouds in the sky. It rained and rained **and rained.**

The King and the Queen looked out, and wondered.

And the Princess, with a smile as bright as a rainbow, stood on top of the hill and sang:

Enough is enough and not one stitch more.